He

This book is written by Yorkshire Dalesman columnist, and former Dales auctioneer, Bryan Thompson. The wonderful illustrations that bring this book to life are by the talented Helen Crowder.

Herby is a real-life tortoise that belongs to Bryan's daughter and grandchildren up on 'Windy Hill' - a colloquial name for Swincliffe Top near Hampsthwaite.

The book is based on the actual three-week disappearance of Herby, and the adventures that we suspect the naughty little scamp may have embarked upon during his travels.

The book is dedicated to Bryan's granddaughter, the wonderful and ever-smiling Connie Clare... our little ray of sunshine x

Herby's Run

Story by Bryan Thompson, illustrations by Helen Crowder

Herby

Herby the tortoise lived at Windy Hill, in a little cottage at the peak of Swincliffe Top, just outside Hampsthwaite village. He lived there with his forever family of Dan the dad, Emma the mum, Finlay the growing boy of teen years, and Connie Clare the bright eyed star of Hampsthwaite Primary School. Jet, the black Labrador, mum of seven mischievous pups, also lived in the little country cottage and would come out into the green grassed garden to snuffle and nudge Herby in welcome. Herby had a comfy, safely fenced, part of the garden with his little house for shelter, a little pond to bathe in and a big pile of tender lettuce and dandelion leaves to munch on.

Herby's house

Then, one day, when Herby was in his safe little pen munching on his favourite leaves he noticed that his front door had blown open so he went off to explore the wide open space of the back garden. There was nobody about, Daddy Dan was at work, Mummy

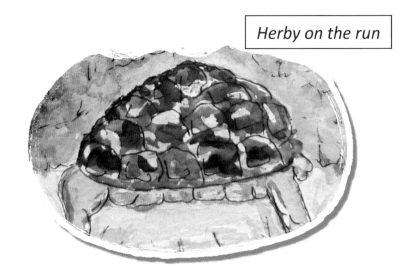

Emma was on holiday with the girls, Finlay was studying at Rosset school and Connie Clare was enjoying her lunch at Hampsthwaite Primary School. So off he scuttled to examine the flower beds and the apple trees, munching a few leaves from the petunias as he passed, watched by his friend, Jet the black Labrador, who had seen him come out of his house as she looked out of her window.

Tortoises can run surprisingly fast when they see something that they want and Herby scuttled with all his might across the green lawn, as he spied some tasty looking carrot fronds waving to him in the breeze from their neat little beds in the vegetable garden. He rushed to the tasty morsels and eagerly snaffled up the green tops, then chewed on the succulent little carrots as they were swiftly unearthed by his tugging.

The warm sun shone on his shiny shell and he smacked his little lips in enjoyment of the freedom and comfort of the day. Finishing his snack he cast his gaze about the neat country garden to see who else might be around...

Herby looks around...

Seeing his friend the horse who lived in the field next door Herby scuttled over to say hello to him...

Herby's friend

As he went along to say hello, Herby saw that there was a hole in the fence that he could just squeeze through and he went into the open grass field with his large friend the horse. But the horse clumped about with his big hooves and Herby was frightened that he might be squashed so off he went, away out, into the meadow smelling and tasting the fresh green grass shoots and fragrant herbs as he sped along.

Suddenly a strange bleating noise made him stop and lift his head in amazement as he saw a mummy sheep and her little lamb.

Mummy sheep and baby lamb...

Mummy sheep are usually very friendly visitors, but when the are looking after their little flock of lambs, they can sometimes become quite protective, and will give a little stamp of their hoof to warn off any intruders. Herby knew this and so he just gave a polite nod and smile as he kept moving along...

The dark and wild, Gormires Wood!

Passing the sheep, Herby came to the edge of the dark and wild... Gormires Wood! Being a strong and brave tortoise, Herby went along the edge of the wood and could hear strange noises coming from within the woods, as the old trees creaked in the wind, and a the animals forged in the undergrowth.

Herby had a mind to venture into the wood, but was distracted by the sound of laughter just around the corner...

Herby continued along the woodland edge, where he met Percy goose and Percy's two sisters as they bathed in their blue pond.

The geese were delighted, splashing and cackling with the pleasure of meeting Herby and whistling to him as he had a long cool drink from the clear stream that fed the pond with sparkling water.

Herby meets Percy Goose and his two sisters...

Herby felt that he had found a true friend in Percy Goose as they laughed together whilst playing in the water, and knew that their adventures together would blossom. But for now, Herby had further adventures on his own and continued his journey...

Around the corner he went on, enjoying the exercise as he stretched his little legs. Then he saw some pretty flowers and sitting amongst them was a floppy eared furry animal which was, of course, a bunny rabbit... sunning herself and stamping her feet thinking that this stranger might be dangerous! She soon realised that Herby was a friend and so he stayed a while in the sun with her and her to share a few munches on the grass together.

Herby meets Mrs Rabbit

After filling his tummy with the lovely green grass and few dandelion leaves, they said goodbye and Mrs Rabbit watched intently as Herby went on his way, on to his next adventure...

Herby was happy day-dreaming in the warm sunshine, as he gently trundled on his way. In fact he was so happy in his own thoughts, that he didn't even notice the spiky rolled up ball right until the moment when he bumped into it!

The strange object prickled his nose as he went up to it and smelled it closely. He jumped back in fright as the ball opened out to reveal a feisty hedgehog who grumped and squeaked at him for spoiling her afternoons nap so that she would be ready for the long night seeking her dinner.

Spiky the hedgehog

Soon Mrs Hedgehog forgave him and gave him a friendly smile as he went on through the hedge and into the wild wood itself.

It was dark and damp in the thick wood with large overhanging trees and heaps of rotting leaves so Herby pressed on quickly down the well trodden gamekeepers path to try and find the sun again. Then, he heard a snuffling and a snapping of teeth from behind him, Herby was frightened, so he moved as fast as his little legs would go, but not fast enough as hungry Mr. Fox soon caught up with him!

The hungry Mr. Fox

The very big fox with a shiny red fur coat and a large bushy tail was quite hungry, and he jumped on poor little Herby who immediately retreated inside his safe and sound shell to hide!

Mr. Fox was flummoxed by this animal as he had never seen a tortoise before and was used to gobbling up tasty hens so he had a nibble and chew on the back of Herby's strong hard shell but this hurt his teeth so let go and dropped Herby on the floor. What a relief! Herby was too tough for hungry Mr.Fox! Most disgruntled Mr.Fox nudged Herby around with is nose, before giving up and scuttling off to his lair in the deep depths of Gormires Wood, looking for his next prey.

Herby was now quite disorientated and lost! He wandered deeper into the wood as darkness fell and had to keep wandering for several long nights looking for his safe home and his friends who lived there.

Herby nestled under a bed of leaves...

Alone and afraid in the glimmering moonlight Herby shivered under the cover of a few leaves as he took refuge in the woods for the night and slept quietly as he dreamed of home...

Back at Windy Hill his friends were desperately searching for him, with his picture appearing on the worldwide web and an 'all points alert' was put out for the errant tortoise who had wandered off from a previous home and obviously had a naughty past!

Just then, Herby was awoken from his peaceful slumber, as a new voice called to him with a twit-twooing whistling call from way up in the trees...

It was Barney the barn owl who had spotted his old friend from the Windy Hill garden. Barney often sat in the apple tree at Windy Hill, looking for mice and rats for his supper and would frequently see Herby in his warm safe home. Barney flew silently down and whistled to Herby who followed his insistent calls as he led him to the outer edge of the wood.

Herby's little face lit up with joy as he climbed out through the ditch that surrounded the wood and across the grass verge, then onto the busy road with no thought of the danger from the fast cars!

Fortunately a kind lady spotted him and recognised him from the web, she gathered him up and returned him to his family on Windy Hill where he was soon back in his nice big run with the gate securely fastened, along with a giant heap of dandelion leaves and lettuce to munch on as he hadn't eaten for days! Herby gobbled them all up and was very content.

Yay! Herby is home!

And so ended Herby's Run... home once more.

The End.

Illustrations by Helen Crowder...

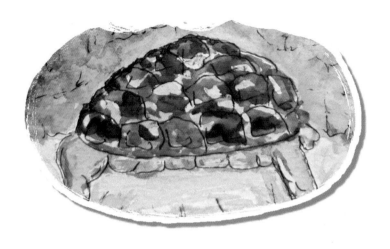

Printed in Great Britain
by Amazon

83269789R00016